W9-DGA-144

THE ANSWER

BOOKS BY **PHILIP WYLIE**

HEAVY LADEN

BABES AND SUCKLINGS

GLADIATOR

THE MURDERER INVISIBLE

FOOTPRINT OF CINDERELLA

THE SAVAGE GENTLEMAN

FINNLEY WREN: HIS NOTIONS AND OPINIONS

AS THEY REVELED

TOO MUCH OF EVERYTHING

AN APRIL AFTERNOON

THE BIG ONES GET AWAY

SALT WATER DAFFY

THE OTHER HORSEMAN

GENERATION OF VIPERS

CORPSES AT INDIAN STONES

FISH AND TIN FISH

NIGHT UNTO NIGHT

AN ESSAY ON MORALS

CRUNCH AND DES: STORIES OF FLORIDA FISHING

OPUS 21

THE DISAPPEARANCE

THREE TO BE READ

DENIZENS OF THE DEEP

TOMORROW!

TREASURE CRUISE AND OTHER CRUNCH AND DES STORIES

THE ANSWER

THE INNOCENT AMBASSADORS

and

THE ARMY WAY by Philip Wylie and William W. Muir

THE ANSWER

PHILIP WYLIE

HOLT, RINEHART AND WINSTON, NEW YORK

For
MARY TAY and SAM PRYOR
with love

THE ANSWER

FIFTEEN minutes!" . . . The loud-speakers blared on the flight deck, boomed below, and murmured on the bridge where the brass was assembling. The length of the carrier was great. Consonants from distant horns came belatedly to every ear, and metal fabric set up echoes besides. So the phrase stuttered through the ship and over the sea. Fifteen minutes to the bomb test.

Major General Marcus Scott walked to the cable railing around the deck and looked at the very blue morning. The ship's engines had stopped and she lay still, aimed west toward the target island like an arrow in a drawn bow.

Men passing saluted. The general returned the salutes, bringing a weathered hand to a lofty forehead, to straight, coal-black hair above gray eyes and the hawk nose of an Indian.

His thoughts veered to the weather. The far surface of the Pacific was lavender; the nearby water, seen deeper, a lucent violet. White clouds passed gradually—clouds much of a size and shape —with cobalt avenues between. The general, to whom the sky was more familiar than the sea, marveled at that mechanized appearance. It was as if some cosmic weather engine—east, and below the Equator—puffed clouds from Brobdingnagian stacks and sent them rolling over the earth, as

9

regular and even-spaced as the white snorts of a climbing locomotive.

He put away the image. Such fantasy belonged in another era, when he had been a young man at West Point, a brilliant young man, more literary than military, a young man fascinated by the "soldier poets" of the first World War. The second, which he had helped to command in the air, produced no romanticists. Here a third war was in the making, perhaps, a third that might put an end to poetry forever.

"Ten minutes! All personnel complete checks, take assigned stations for test!"

General Scott went across the iron deck on scissoring legs that seemed to hurry the tall man without themselves hurrying. Sailors had finished stringing the temporary cables which, should a freak buffet from the H-bomb reach the area, would prevent them from being tossed overboard. They were gathering, now, to watch. Marc Scott entered the carrier's island and hastened to the bridge on turning steps of metal, not using the shined brass rail.

Admiral Stanforth was there—anvil shoulders, marble hair, feldspar complexion. Pouring coffee for Senator Blaine with a good-host chuckle and that tiger look in the corners of his eyes. "Morning, Marc! Get any sleep at all?" He gave the general no time to answer. "This is General Scott, gentlemen. In charge of today's drop. Commands base on Sangre Islands. Senator Blaine——"

The senator had the trappings of office: the *embonpoint* and shrewd eyes, the pince-nez on a ribbon, the hat with the wide brim that meant a Western or Southern senator. He had the William Jennings Bryan voice. But these were for his constituents.

The man who used the voice said genuinely, "General, I'm honored. Your record in the Eighth Air Force is one we're almost too proud of to mention in front of you."

"Thank you, sir."

"You know Doctor Trumbul?"

Trumbul was thin and thirty, an all-brown scholar whose brown eyes were so vivid the rest seemed but a background for his eyes. His hand clasped Scott's. "All too well! I flew with Marc Scott when we dropped Thermonuclear Number Eleven—on a parachute!"

There was some laughter; they knew about that near-disastrous test.

"How's everybody at Los Alamos?" the general asked.

The physicist shrugged. "Same. They'll feel better later today—if this one comes up to expectations."

The admiral was introducing again. "Doctor Antheim, general. Antheim's from MIT. He's also the best amateur magician I ever saw perform. Too bad you came aboard so late last night."

Antheim was as quietly composed as a family physician—a big man in a gray suit.

"Five minutes!" the loud-speaker proclaimed.

You could see the lonely open ocean, the sky, the cumulus clouds. But the target island—five miles long and jungle-painted—lay over the horizon. An island created by volcanic cataclysm millions of years ago and destined this day to vanish in a man-patented calamity. Somewhere a hundred thousand feet above, Scott's own ship, a B-111, was moving at more than seven hundred miles an hour, closing on an imaginary point from which, along an imaginary line, a big bomb would curve earthward, never to hit, but utterly to devastate. You could not see his B-111 and you would probably not even see the high, far-off tornadoes of smoke when, the bomb away, she let go with her rockets to hurtle off even faster from the expanding sphere of blast.

"Personally," Antheim, the MIT scientist, was saying to General Larsen, "it's my feeling that whether or not your cocker is a fawning type depends on your attitude as a dog owner. I agree, all cockers have Saint Bernard appetites. Nevertheless,

I'm sold on spaniels. In all the field trials last autumn——"

Talking about dogs. Well, why not? Random talk was the best antidote for tension, for the electrically counted minutes that stretched unbearably because of their measurement. Scott had a dog—his kids had one, rather: Pompey, the mutt, whose field trials took place in the yards and playgrounds of Baltimore, Maryland, in the vicinity of Millbrook Road. He wondered what would be happening at home—where Ellen would be at—he calculated time belts, the hour-wide, orange-peel-shaped sections into which man had carved his planet. Be evening on Millbrook Road——

John Farrier arrived—Farrier, of the great Farrier Corporation. His pale blue eyes looked out over the ship's flat deck toward the west, the target. But he was saying to somebody, in his crisp yet not uncourteous voice, "I consider myself something of a connoisseur in the matter of honey. We have our own apiary at Hobe Sound. Did you ever taste antidesma honey? Or the honey gathered from palmetto flowers?"

"Two minutes!"

The count-down was the hardest part of a weapons test. What went before was work—sheer work, detailed, exhausting. But what came after had excitements, real and potential, like hazardous exploring, the general thought; you never knew precisely what would ensue. Not precisely.

Tension, Scott repeated to himself. And he thought, *Why do I feel sad? Is it prescience of failure? Will we finally manage to produce a dud?*

Fatigue, he answered himself. Setting up this one had been a colossal chore. They called it Bugaboo—Operation Bugaboo in Test Series Avalanche. Suddenly he wished Bugaboo wouldn't go off.

"One minute! All goggles in place! Exposed personnel without goggles, sit down, turn backs toward west, cover eyes with hands!"

Before he blacked out the world, he took a last look at the sky, the sea—and the sailors, wheeling, sitting, covering their eyes. Then he put on the goggles. The obsidian lenses brought absolute dark. From habit, he cut his eyes back and forth to make certain there was no leak of light—light that could damage the retina.

"Ten seconds!"

The ship drew a last deep breath and held it. In an incredibly long silence, the general mused on thousands upon thousands of other men in other ships, ashore and in the air, who now were also holding back breathing.

"Five!"

An imbecile notion flickered in the general's brain and expired: He could leap up and cry

"Stop!" He still could. A word from Stanforth. A button pressed. The whole shebang would chute on down, unexploded. And umpteen million dollars' worth of taxpayers' money would be wasted by that solitary syllable of his.

"Four!"

Still, the general thought, his lips smiling, his heart frozen, why should they—or anybody—*be doing this?*"

"Three seconds . . . two . . . one . . . zero!"

Slowly, the sky blew up.

On the horizon, a supersun grabbed up degrees of diameter and rose degrees. The sea, ship, praying sailors became as plain as they had been bare-eyed in full sun, then plainer still. Eyes, looking through the inky glass, saw the universe stark white. A hundred-times-sun-sized sun mottled itself with lesser whiteness, bulked up, became the perfect sphere, ascending hideously and setting forth on the Pacific a molten track from ship to livid self. Tumors of light more brilliant than the sun sprang up on the mathematical sphere; yet these, less blazing than the fireball, appeared as blacknesses.

The thing swelled and swelled and rose; nonetheless, instant miles of upthrust were diminished by the expansion. Abruptly, it exploded around itself a white lewd ring, a halo.

For a time there was no air beneath it, only the

rays and neutrons in vacuum. The atmosphere beyond—incandescent, compressed harder than steel —moved toward the spectators. No sound.

The fireball burned within itself and around itself, burnt the sea away—a hole in it—and a hole in the planet. It melted part way, lopsided, threw out a cubic mile of fire this way—a scarlet asteroid, that.

To greet the birthing of a new, brief star, the regimental sky hung a bunting on every cloud. The mushroom formed quietly, immensely and in haste; it towered, spread, and the incandescent air hurtled at the watchers on the circumferences. In the mushroom new fire burst forth, cubic miles of phosphor-pale flame. The general heard Antheim sigh. That would be the "igniter effect," the new thing, to set fire, infinitely, in the wake of the fire blown out by the miles-out blast. A hellish bit of physics.

Again, again, again the thorium-lithium pulse! Each time—had it been other than jungle and sea; had it been a city, Baltimore—the urban tinder, and the people, would have hair-fired in the debris.

The mushroom climbed on its stalk, the ten-mile circle of what had been part of earth. It split the atmospheric layers and reached for the purple dark, that the flying general knew, where the real sun was also unbearably bright.

Mouths agape, goggles now dangling, the men

on the bridge of the Ticonderoga could look naked-eyed at the sky's exploded rainbows and seething prismatics.

"Stand by for the blast wave!"

It came like the shadow of eclipse. The carrier shuddered. Men sagged, spun on their bottoms. The general felt the familiar compression, a thousand boxing gloves, padded but hitting squarely every part of his body at once.

Then Antheim and Trumbul were shaking hands.

"Congratulations! That ought to be—about it!"

It for what? The enemy? A city? Humanity?

"Magnificent," said Senator Blaine. He added, "We seem O.K."

"Good thing too," a voice laughed. "A dozen of the best sets of brains in America, right in this one spot."

The general thought about that. Two of the world's leading nuclear physicists, the ablest member of the Joint Chiefs of Staff, a senator wise for all his vaudeville appearance, an unbelievably versatile industrialist, the Navy's best tactician. Good brains. But what an occupation for human brains!

Unobtrusively he moved to the iron stairs—the "ladder." Let the good brains and the sight-seers gape at the kaleidoscope aloft. He hurried to his assigned office.

An hour later he had received the important reports.

His B-111 was back on the field, "hot," but not dangerous; damaged, but not severely; the crew in good shape. Celebrating, Major Stokely had bothered to add.

Two drones lost; three more landed in unapproachable condition. One photo recon plane had been hit by a flying chunk of something eighteen miles from ground zero and eight minutes—if the time was right—after the blast. Something that had been thrown mighty high or somehow remained aloft a long while. Wing damage and radioactivity; but, again, no personnel injured.

Phones rang. Messengers came—sailors— quick, quiet, polite. The Ticonderoga was moving, moving swiftly, in toward the place where nothing was, in under the colored bomb clouds.

He had a sensation that something was missing, that more was to be done, that news awaited— which he attributed again to tiredness. Tiredness: what a general was supposed never to feel—and the burden that settled on every pair of starred shoulders. He sighed and picked up the book he had read in empty spaces of the preceding night: Thoreau's "Walden Pond."

Why had he taken Thoreau on this trip? He knew the answer. To be as far as possible, in one way, from the torrent of technology in mid-Pacific; to be as close as possible to a proper view of Atomic-Age Man, in a different way. But now he closed the book as if it had blank pages. After all, Thoreau couldn't take straight Nature, himself; a couple of years beside his pond and he went back to town and lived in Emerson's back yard. For the general that was an aggrieved and aggrieving thought.

Lieutenant Tobey hurried in from the next office. "Something special on TLS. Shall I switch it?"

His nerves tightened. He had expected "something special" on his most restricted wire, without a reason for the expectation. He picked up the instrument when the light went red. "Scott here."

"Rawson. Point L 15."

"Right." That would be instrument site near the mission school on Tempest Island.

"Matter of Import Z." Which meant an emergency.

"I see." General Scott felt almost relieved. Something was wrong; to know even that was better than to have a merely mystifying sense of wrongness.

Rawson—Major Dudley Rawson, the general's cleverest Intelligence officer, simply said, "Import Z, and, I'd say, General, the Z Grade."

"Can't clarify?"

"No, sir."

General Scott marveled for a moment at the tone of Rawson's voice: it was high and the syllables shook. He said, "Right, Raw. Be over." He leaned back in his chair and spoke to the lieutenant, "Would you get me Captain Elverson? I'd like a whirlybird ride."

The helicopter deposited the general in the center of the playing field where the natives at the mission school learned American games. Rawson and two others were waiting. The general gave the customary grateful good-by to his naval escort; then waited for the racket of the departing helicopter to diminish.

He observed that Major Rawson, a lieutenant he did not know and a technical sergeant were soaked with perspiration. But that scarcely surprised him; the sun was now high and the island steamed formidably.

Rawson said, "I put it through Banjo, direct to you, sir. Took the liberty. There's been a casualty."

"Lord!" The general shook his head. "Who?"

"I'd rather show you, sir." The major's eyes traveled to the road that led from the field, through banyan trees, toward the mission. Corrugated-metal roofs sparkled behind the trees, and on the road in the shade a jeep waited.

The general started for the vehicle. "Just give me what particulars you can——"

"I'd rather you saw—it—for yourself."

General Scott climbed into the car, sat, looked closely at the major.

He'd seen funk, seen panic. This was that—and more. The three men sweated like horses, yet they were pallid. They shook—and made no pretense of hiding or controlling it. A "casualty"—and they were soldiers! No casualty could——

"You said 'it,'" the general said. "Just what——"

"For the love of God, don't ask me to explain! It's just behind the mission buildings." Major Rawson tapped the sergeant's shoulder, "Can you drive O.K., Sam?"

The man jerked his head and started the motor. The jeep moved.

The general had impressions of buildings, or brown boys working in a banana grove, and native girls flapping along in such clothes as missionaries consider moral. Then they entered a colonnade of tree trunks which upheld the jungle canopy.

He was afraid in some new way. He must not show it. He concentrated on seeming not to concentrate.

The jeep stopped. Panting slightly, Rawson stepped out, pushed aside the fronds of a large fern tree and hurried along a leafy tunnel. "Little glade up here. That's where the casualty dropped."

"Who found—it?"

"The missionary's youngest boy. Kid named Ted. His dad too. The padre—or whatever the Devoted Brethren call 'em."

The glade appeared—a clear pool of water bordered by terrestrial orchids. A man lay in their way, face down, his clerical collar unbuttoned, his arms extended, hands clasped, breath issuing in hoarse groans.

From maps, memoranda, somewhere, the general remembered the man's name. "You mean Reverend Simms is the victim?" he asked in amazement.

"No," said Rawson; "up ahead." He led the general around the bole of a jacaranda tree. "There."

For a speechless minute the general stood still. On the ground, almost at his feet, in the full sunshine, lay the casualty.

"Agnostic," the general had been called by many; "mystic," by more; "natural philosopher," by devoted chaplains who had served with him. But he was not a man of orthodox religion.

What lay on the fringe of purple flowers was recognizable. He could not, would not, identify it aloud.

Behind him, the major, the lieutenant and the sergeant were waiting shakily for him to name it. Near them, prostrate on the earth, was the missionary—who had already named it and commenced to worship.

It was motionless. The beautiful human face slept in death; the alabastrine body was relaxed in death; the unimaginable eyes were closed and the immense white wings were folded. It was an angel.

The general could bring himself to say, in a soft voice, only, "It looks like one."

The three faces behind him were distracted. "It's an angel," Rawson said in a frantic tone. "And everything we've done, and thought, and believed is nuts! Science is nuts! Who knows, now, what the next move will be?"

The sergeant had knelt and was crossing himself. A babble of repentance issued from his lips— as if he were at confessional. Seeing the general's eyes on him, he interrupted himself to murmur, "I was brought up Catholic." Then, turning back to the figure, with the utmost fright, he crossed himself and went on in a compulsive listing of his sad misdemeanors.

The lieutenant, a buck-toothed young man, was now laughing in a morbid way. A way that was the sure prelude to hysteria.

"Shut up!" the general said; then strode to the figure among the flowers and reached down for its pulse.

At that, Reverend Simms made a sound near to a scream and leaped to his feet. His garments were stained with the black humus in which he had lain; his clerical collar flapped loosely at his neck.

"Don't you even touch it! Heretic! You are not fit to be here! You—and your martial kind—your scientists! Do you not yet see what you have done? Your last infernal bomb has shot down Gabriel, angel of the Lord! This is the end of the world!" His voice tore his throat. "And you are responsible! You are the destroyers!"

The general could not say but that every word the missionary had spoken was true. The beautiful being might indeed be Gabriel. Certainly it was an unearthly creature. The general felt a tendency, if not to panic, at least to take seriously the idea that he was now dreaming or had gone mad. Human hysteria, however, was a known field, and one with which he was equipped to deal.

He spoke sharply, authoritatively, somehow keeping his thoughts a few syllables ahead of his ringing voice, "Reverend Simms, I am a soldier in charge here. If your surmise is correct, God will be my judge. But you have not examined this pathetic victim. That is neither human nor Christian. Suppose it is only hurt, and needs medical attention? What sort of Samaritans would we be, then, to let it perish here in the heat? You may also be mistaken, and that would be a greater cruelty. Suppose it is not what you so logically assume? Suppose it merely happens to be a creature like ourselves, from some real but different planet—thrown, say, from its space-voyaging vehicle by the violence of the morning test?"

The thought, rushing into the general's mind from nowhere, encouraged him. He was at that time willing to concede the likelihood that he stood in the presence of a miracle—and a miracle of the most horrifying sort, since the angel was seemingly dead. But to deal with men, with their minds, and even his own thought process, he needed a less appalling possibility to set alongside apparent fact. If he were to accept the miracle, he would be obliged first to alter his own deep and hard-won faith, along with its corollaries—and that would mean a change in the general's very personality. It would take pain, and time. Meanwhile there were men to deal with —men in mortal frenzy.

The missionary heard him vaguely, caught the suggestion that the general might doubt the being on the ground to be Gabriel, and burst into grotesque, astounding laughter. He rushed from the glade.

After his antic departure, the general said grimly, "That man has about lost his mind! A stupid way to behave, if what he believes is the case!" Then, in drill-sergeant tones, he barked, "Sergeant! Take a leg. . . . Lieutenant, the other. . . . Rawson, help me here."

He took gentle hold. The flesh, if it was flesh, felt cool, but not yet cold. When he lifted, the shoulder turned easily; it was less heavy than he had expected. The other men, slowly, dubiously, took stations and drew nerving breaths.

"See to it, men," the general ordered—as if it were mere routine and likely to be overlooked by second-rate soldiers—"that those wings don't drag on the ground! Let's go!"

He could observe and think a little more analytically as they carried the being toward the jeep. The single garment worn by the angel was snow-white and exquisitely pleated. The back and shoulder muscles were obviously of great power, and constructed to beat the great wings. They were, he gathered, operational wings, not vestigial. Perhaps the creature came from a small planet where gravity was so slight that these wings sufficed for flying about. That was at least thinkable.

A different theory which he entertained briefly —because he was a soldier—seemed impossible on close scrutiny. The creature they carried from the glade was not a fake—not some biological device of the enemy fabricated to startle the Free World. What they were carrying could not have been man-made, unless the Reds had moved centuries ahead of everyone else in the science of biology. This was no hybrid. The angel had lived, grown, moved its wings and been of one substance.

It filled the back seat of the jeep. The general said, "I'll drive. . . . Lieutenant . . . Sergeant, meet me at the field. . . . Raw, you get HQ again on a Z line and have them send a helicopter. Two extra passengers for the trip out, tell them. Have General Budford fly in now, if possible. Give no information except that these suggestions are from me."

"Yes, sir."

"Then black out all communications from this island."

"Yes, sir."

"If the Devoted Brethren Mission won't shut its radio off, see that it stops working."

The major nodded, waited a moment, and walked down the jungle track in haunted obedience.

"I'll drive it," the general repeated.

He felt long and carefully for a pulse. Nothing. The body was growing rigid. He started the jeep. Once he glanced back at his incredible companion. The face was perfectly serene; the lurching of the vehicle, for all his care in driving, had parted the lips.

He reached the shade at the edge of the playing field where the jeep had first been parked. He cut the motor. The school compound had been empty of persons when he passed this time. There had been no one on the road; not even any children. Presently the mission bell began to toll slowly. Reverend Simms, he thought, would be holding services. That probably explained the absence of people, the hush in the heat of midday, the jade quietude.

He pulled out a cigarette, hesitated to smoke it. He wondered if there were any further steps which he should take. For his own sake, he again carefully examined the angel, and he was certain afterward only that it was like nothing earthly, that it could be an angel and that it had died, without any external trace of the cause. Concussion, doubtless.

He went over his rationalizations. If men with wings like this did exist on some small, remote planet; if any of them had visited Earth in rocket ships in antiquity, it would explain a great deal about what he had thitherto called "superstitious" beliefs. Fiery chariots, old prophets being taken to heaven by angels, and much else.

If the Russians had "made" it and dropped it to confuse the Free World, then it was all over; they were already too far ahead scientifically.

He lighted the cigarette. Deep in the banyans, behind the screens of thick, aerial roots and oval leaves, a twig snapped. His head swung fearfully. He half expected another form—winged, clothed in light—to step forth and demand the body of its fallen colleague.

A boy emerged—a boy of about nine, suntanned, big-eyed and muscular in the stringy way of boys. He wore only a T-shirt and shorts; both bore marks of his green progress through the jungle.

"You have it," he said. Not accusatively. Not even very emotionally. "Where's father?"

"Are you——"

"I'm Ted Simms." The brown gaze was suddenly excited. "And you're a general!"

The man nodded. "General Scott." He smiled. "You've seen"—he moved his head gently toward the rear seat—"my passenger before?"

"I saw him fall. I was there, getting Aunt Cora a bunch of flowers."

The general remained casual, in tone of voice, "Tell me about it."

"Can I sit in the jeep? I never rode in one yet."

"Sure."

The boy climbed in, looked intently at the angel, and sat beside the general. He sighed. "Sure is handsome, an angel," said the boy. "I was just up there at the spring, picking flowers, because Aunt Cora likes flowers quite a lot, and she was mad because I didn't do my arithmetic well. We had seen the old test shot, earlier, and we're sick and tired of them, anyhow! They scare the natives and make them go back to their old, heathen customs. Well, I heard this whizzing up in the air, and down it came, wings out, trying to fly, but only spiraling, sort of. Like a bird with an arrow through it. You've seen that kind of wobbly flying?"

"Yes."

"It came down. It stood there a second and then it sat."

"Sat?" The general's lips felt dry. He licked them. "Did it—see you?"

"See me? I was right beside it."

The boy hesitated and the general was on the dubious verge of prodding when the larklike voice continued, "It sat there crying for a while."

"Crying!"

"Of course. The H-bomb must of hurt it something awful. It was crying. You could hear it sobbing and trying to get its breath even before it touched the ground. It cried, and then it looked at me and it stopped crying and it smiled. It had a real wonderful smile when it smiled."

The boy paused. He had begun to look with fascination at the dashboard instruments.

"Then what?" the general murmured.

"Can I switch on the lights?" He responded eagerly to the nod and talked as he switched the lights, tried the horn. "Then not much. It smiled and I didn't know what to do. I never saw an angel before. Father says he knows people who have, though. So I said 'Hello,' and it said 'Hello,' and it said, after a minute or so, 'I was a little too late,' and tears got in its eyes again and it leaned back and kind of tucked in its wings and, after a while, it died."

"You mean the—angel—spoke to you—in English?"

"Don't they know all languages?" the boy asked, smiling.

"I couldn't say," the general replied. "I suppose they do."

He framed another question, and heard a sharp "Look out!" There was a thwack in the foliage. Feet ran. A man grunted. He threw himself in front of the boy.

Reverend Simms had crept from the banyan, carrying a shotgun, intent, undoubtedly, on preventing the removal of the unearthly being from his island. The lieutenant and sergeant, rounding a turn in the road, had seen him, thrown a stone to divert him, and rushed him. There was almost no scuffle.

The general jumped down from the jeep, took the gun, looked into the missionary's eyes and saw no sanity there—just fury and bafflement.

"You've had a terrible shock, Dominie," he said, putting the gun in the front of the jeep. "We all have. But this is a thing for the whole world, if it's what you believe it to be. Not just for here and now and you. We shall have to take it away and ascertain——"

"Ye of little faith!" the missionary intoned.

The general pitied the man and suddenly envied him; it was comforting to be so sure about anything.

Comforting. But was such comfort valid or was it specious? He looked toward the jeep. Who could doubt now?

He could. It was his way of being—to doubt at first. It was also his duty, as he saw duty.

Rawson, looking old and deathly ill, came down the cart track in the green shadows. But he had regained something of his manner. "All set, Marc. No word will leave here. Plane's on the way; General Budford's flying in himself. Old Bloodshed said it better be Z priority." The major eyed the white, folded wings. "I judge he'll be satisfied."

General Scott grinned slightly. "Have a cigarette, Raw." He sat beside the praying missionary with some hope of trying to bring the man's mind from dread and ecstasy back to the human problems—the awesome, unpredictable human enigmas —which would be involved by this "casualty."

One thing was sure. The people who had felt for years that man didn't yet know enough to experiment with the elemental forces of Nature were going to feel entirely justified when this story rocked the planet.

If, the general thought on with a sudden, icy feeling, it wasn't labeled Top Secret and concealed forever.

That could be. The possibility appalled him. He looked up angrily at the hot sky. No bomb effects were visible here; only the clouds' cyclorama toiling across the blue firmament. Plenty of Top Secrets up there still, he thought.

The President of the United States was awakened after a conference. When they told him, he reached for his dressing gown, started to get up and then sat on the edge of his bed. "Say that again."

They said it again.

The President's white hair was awry, his eyes had the sleep-hung look of a man in need of more rest. His brain, however, came wide awake.

"Let me have that in the right sequence. The Bugaboo test brought down, on Tempest Island, above Salandra Strait, an angel—or something that looked human and had wings, anyhow. Who's outside and who brought that over?"

His aide, Smith, said, "Weatherby, Colton and Dwane."

The Secretary of State. The chairman of the Joint Chiefs of Staff. The chairman of the Atomic Energy Commission.

"Sure of communications? Could be a terrific propaganda gag. The Reds could monkey with our wave lengths——" The President gestured, put on the dressing gown.

"Quadruple-checked. Budford talked on the scrambler. Also Marc Scott, who made the first investigation of the—er—casualty." Smith's peaceful, professorish face was composed, still, but his eyes were wrong.

"Good men."

"None better. Admiral Stanforth sent independent verification. Green, of AEC, reported in on Navy and Air Force channels. Captain Wilmot, ranking Navy chaplain out there, swore it was a genuine angel. It must be—something, Mr. President! Something all right!"

"Where is it now?"

"On the way, naturally. Scott put it aboard a B-111. Due in here by three o'clock. Coffee waiting in the office."

"I'll go out, Clem. Get the rest of the Cabinet up and here. The rest of the JCS. Get Ames at CIA. This thing has got to stay absolutely restricted till we know more."

"Of course."

"Scott with it?"

"Budford." Smith smiled. "Ranked Scott. Some mission, hunh? An angel. Imagine!"

"All my life I've been a God-fearing man," the President replied. "But I can't imagine. We'll wait till it's here." He started toward the door where other men waited tensely. He paused. "Whatever it is, it's the end to—what has been, these last fifteen years. And that's a good thing." The President smiled.

It was, perhaps, the longest morning in the history of the capital. Arrangements had been made for the transportation of the cargo secretly but swiftly from the airfield to the White House. A select but celebrated group of men had been chosen to examine the cargo. They kept flying in to Washington and arriving in limousines all morning. But they did not know why they had been summoned. Reporters could not reach a single Cabinet member. No one available at State or the Pentagon, at AEC or CIA could give any information at all. So there were merely conjectures, which led to rumors:

Something had gone wrong with an H-bomb.

The President had been assassinated.

Russia had sent an ultimatum.

Hitler had reappeared.

Toward the end of that morning, a call came which the President took in person. About thirty men watched his face, and all of them became afraid.

When he hung up he said unsteadily, "Gentlemen, the B-111 flying it in is overdue at San Francisco and presumed down at sea. All agencies have commenced a search. I have asked, meantime, that those officers and scientists who saw, examined or had any contact with the—strange being be flown here immediately. Unless they find the plane and recover what it carried, that's all we can do."

"The whole business," Dwane said, after a long silence, "could be a hoax. If the entire work party engaged in Test Series Avalanche formed a conspiracy——"

"Why should they?" asked Weatherby.

"Because, Mr. Secretary," Dwane answered, "a good many people on this globe think mankind has carried this atomic-weapons business too far."

General Colton smiled. "I can see a few frightened men conspiring against the world and their own government, with some half-baked idealistic motive. But not a fleet and an army. Not, for that matter, Stanforth or Scott. Not Scott. Not a hoax."

"They'll report here tonight, gentlemen, in any case." The President walked to a window and looked out at the spring green of a lawn and the budding trees above. "We'll know then what they learned, at least. Luncheon?"

On the evening of the third day afterward, Marc Scott greeted the President formally in his office. At the President's suggestion they went out together, in the warm April twilight, to a low-walled terrace.

"The reason I asked you to come to the White House again," the President began, "was to talk to you entirely alone. I gathered, not from your words, but from your manner at recent meetings, General, that you had some feelings about this matter."

"Feelings, Mr. President?" He had feelings. But would the statesman understand or regard them as naïve, as childish?

The President chuckled and ran his fingers through his thick white hair in a hesitant way that suggested he was uncertain of himself. "I have a fearful decision to make." He sighed and was silent for several seconds as he watched the toy silhouettes of three jet planes move across the lemon-yellow sky. "There are several courses I can take. I can order complete silence about the whole affair. Perhaps a hundred people know. If I put it on a Top Secret basis, rumors may creep out. But they could be scotched. The world would then be deprived of any real knowledge of your—angel.

"Next, I could take up the matter with the other heads of state. The friendly ones." He paused and then nodded his head unsurely. "Yes. Even the Russians. And the satellite governments. With heaven knows what useful effect! Finally, I could simply announce to the world that you and a handful of others found the body of what appears to have been an angel, and that it was irretrievably lost while being flown to Washington."

Since the President stopped with those words, Marc said, "Yes, sir."

"Three equally poor possibilities. If it was an angel—a divine messenger—and our test destroyed it, I have, I feel, no moral right whatever to keep the world from knowing. Irrespective of any consequences."

"The consequences!" Marc Scott murmured.

"You can imagine them!" The President uncrossed his legs, stretched, felt for a cigarette, took a light from the general. "Tremendous, incalculable, dangerous consequences! All truly and decently religious people would be given a tremendous surge of hope, along with an equal despair over the angel's death and the subsequent loss of the—body. Fanatics would literally go mad. The news could produce panic, civil unrest, bloodshed. And we have nothing to show. No proof. Nothing tangible. The enemy could use the whole story for propaganda in a thousand evil ways. Being atheistic, they would proclaim it an American madness—what you will. Even clergymen, among themselves, are utterly unagreed, when they are told the situation."

"I can imagine."

The President smiled a little and went on, "I called half a dozen leaders to Washington. Cardinal Thrace. Bishop Neuermann. Father Bolder. Reverend Matthews. Every solitary man had a different reaction. When they became assured that I meant precisely what I said, they began a theological battle"—the President chuckled ruefully at the memory—"that went on until they left, and looked good for a thousand years. Whole denominations would split! Most of the clergy, however, agreed on one point: it was not an angel."

The general was startled. "Not an angel? Then, what——"

"Because it died. Because it was killed or destroyed. Angels, General, are immortal. They are not human flesh and blood. No. I think you can say that, by and large, the churches would never assent to the idea that the being you saw was Gabriel or any other angel."

"I hadn't thought of that."

"I had," the President replied. "You are not, General, among the orthodox believers, I take it."

"No, Mr. President."

"So I judged. Well, let me get to my reason for asking you to confer privately with me. The churchmen debated hotly—to use the politest possible phrase—over the subject. But the scientists—whom I also consulted"—he drew a breath and swallowed, like a man whose memory of hard-controlled temper is still painful—"the scientists were at scandalous loggerheads. Two of them actually came to blows! I've heard every theory you can conceive of, and a lot I couldn't. Every idea from the one that you, General, and all the rest of you out in the Pacific, were victims of mass hypnosis and the whole thing's an illusion, to a hundred versions of the 'little men from outer space' angle. In the meeting day before yesterday, however, I noticed you were rather quiet and reserved about expressing any opinion. I've since looked up your record. It's magnificent." The President hesitated.

Marc said nothing.

"You're a brave, brilliant, level-headed, sensitive person, and a man's man. Your record makes a great deal too plain for you to deny out of modesty. You are an exceptional man. In short, you're the very sort of person I'd pick to look into a mere report of an incident of that sort. So what I want—why I asked you here—is your impression. Your feelings. Your reactions at the time. Your reflections since. Your man-to-man, down-to-earth, openhearted emotions about it all—and not more theory, whether theological or allegedly scientific! Do you see?"

The appeal was forceful. Marc felt as if he were all the members of some audiences the President had swayed—all of them in one person, one American citizen—now asked—now all but commanded—to bare his soul. He felt the great, inner power of the President and understood why the people of the nation had chosen him for office.

"I'll tell you," he answered quietly. "For what it's worth. I'm afraid that it is mighty little." He pondered a moment. "First, when I suddenly saw it, I was shocked. Not frightened, Mr. President—though the rest were. Just—startled. When I really looked at the—casualty, I thought, first of all, that it was beautiful. I thought it had, in its dead face, great intelligence and other qualities."

The President rested his hand on the uniformed knee. "That's it, man! The 'other qualities'! What were they?"

Marc exhaled unevenly. "This is risky. It's all —remembered impression. I thought it looked kind. Noble too. Almost, but not exactly, sweet. I thought it had tremendous courage. The kind that—well, I thought of it as roaring through space and danger and unimagined risks to get here. Daring H-bombs. And I thought, Mr. President, one more thing: I thought it had determination—as if there was a gigantic feel about it of—mission."

There was a long silence. Then the President said in a low voice, "That all, Marc?"

"Yes. Yes, sir."

"So I thought." He stood up suddenly, not a man of reflection and unresolved responsibility, but an executive with work ahead. "Mission! We don't know what it was. If only there was something tangible!" He held out his hand and gripped the general with great strength. "I needed that word to decide. We'll wait. Keep it absolutely restricted. There might be another. The message to us, from them, whoever they are, might come in some different way or by more of these messengers! After all,

I cannot represent them to the world—expose this incredible incident—without knowing what the mission was. But to know there was a mission——" He sighed and went on firmly, "When I finally get to bed tonight, I'll sleep, Marc, as I haven't slept since I took office!"

"It's only my guess," the general responded. "I haven't any evidence to explain those feelings."

"You've said enough for me! Thank you, General." Then, to Marc Scott's honor and embarrassment, the President drew himself straight, executed a salute, held it a moment, turned from the terrace and marched alone into the White House.

During the months-long, single day of Northern Siberia's summertime, on a night that had no darkness, a fireball burst suddenly above the arctic rim. As it rose, it turned the tundra blood-red. For a radius of miles the permafrost was hammered down and a vast, charred basin was formed. In the adjacent polar seas ice melted. A mushroom cloud broke through the atmospheric layers with a speed and to a height that would have perplexed, if not horrified, the Free World's nuclear physicists.

In due course, counters the world around would begin to click and the information would be whispered about that the Russians were ahead in the H-bomb field. That information would be thereupon restricted so that the American public would never learn the truth.

In Siberia the next morning awed Soviet technicians—and the most detached nuclear physicists have been awed, even stupefied, by their creations—measured the effects of their new bomb carefully: area of absolute incineration, area of absolute destruction by blast, putative scope of fire storm, radius of penetrative radiation, kinds and concentrations of radioactive fallout, half-lives, dispersion of same, kilos of pressure per square centimeter. Then, on maps of the United States of America, these technicians superimposed tinted circles of colored plastics, so that a glance would show exactly what such a bomb would destroy of Buffalo and environs, St. Paul, Seattle, Dallas, as well as New York, Chicago, Philadelphia, Los Angeles, and so on—the better targets. These maps, indicating the imaginary annihilation of millions, were identical with certain American maps, save for the fact that the latter bore such city names as Moscow, Leningrad, Stalingrad, Vladivostok, Ordzhonikidze, Dnepropetrovsk, and the like.

It was while the technicians were correlating their bomb data—and the sky over the test base was still lava—that coded word came in to the commanding officer of the base concerning a "casualty."

The casualty had been found in dying condition by a peasant who had been ordered to evacuate his sod hut in that region weeks before. After the casualty, he had been summarily shot for disobedience.

The general went to the scene forthwith—and returned a silent, shaken man. Using communication channels intended only for war emergency, he got in touch with Moscow. The premier was not in his offices in the new, forty-six-story skyscraper; but his aides were persuaded to disturb him at one of his suburban villas. They were reluctant; he had retired to the country with Lamenula, the communist Italian actress.

The premier listened to the faint, agitated news from Siberia and said, "The garrison must be drunk."

"I assure you, Comrade——"

"Put Vorshiv on."

Vorshiv said, uneasily, the same thing. Yes, he had seen it. . . . Yes, it had wings. . . . No, it could not be an enemy trick. . . . No, there were no interplanetary vehicles about; nothing on the radar in the nature of an unidentified flying object. . . . Certainly, they had been meticulous in the sky watch; this had been a new type of bomb, incorporating a new principle, and it would never have done to let an enemy reconnaissance plane observe the effects.

"I will come," said the premier.

He ordered a new Khalov-239 prepared for the flight. He was very angry. Lamenula had been coy —and the premier had enjoyed the novelty of that, until the call from Siberia had interrupted. Now he would have to make a long, uncomfortable journey in a jet—which always frightened him a little— and he would be obliged to postpone the furthering of his friendship with the talented, beautiful, honey-haired young Italian.

Night came to the Siberian flatlands and the sky clouded so that there was a semblance of dark-ness. A frigid wind swept from the Pole, freezing the vast area of mud created by the H-bomb. In the morning the premier came in at the base airfield, twelve jets streaming in the icy atmosphere, for-ward rockets blasting to brake the race of the great ship over the hard-packed terrain. It stopped only a few score rods short of the place where the "inade-quate workers" lay buried—the more than ten thou-sand slaves who had died to make the field.

Curiously enough, it was an American jeep which took the premier out to the scrubby patch of firs. The angel lay untouched, but covered with a tarpaulin and prodigiously guarded round about by men and war machines.

"Take it off."

He stood a long time, simply looking, his silent generals and aides beside him.

Not a tall man, this Soviet premier, but broad, overweight, bearlike in fur clothing—a man with a Mongol face and eyes as dark, as inexpressive and unfeeling as prunes. A man whose face was always shiny, as if he exuded minutely a thin oil. A man highly educated by the standards of his land; a man ruthless by any standard in history.

What went through his head as he regarded the dazzling figure, he would not afterward have catalogued. Not in its entirety. He was afraid, of course. He was always afraid. But he had achieved that level of awareness which acknowledges, and uses, fear. In the angel he saw immediately a possible finish to the dreams of Engels, Marx, the rest. He saw a potential end of communism, and even of the human race. This milk-white cadaver, this impossible reality, this beauty Praxiteles could never have achieved even symbolically, could mean—anything.

Aloud, he said—his first remark—"Michelangelo would have appreciated this."

Some of the men around him, scared, breathing steam in the gray, purgatorial morning, smiled or chuckled at their chief's erudition and self-possession. Others agreed solemnly: Michelangelo—

whoever he was or had been—would have appreciated this incredible carcass.

He then went up and kicked the foot of the angel with his own felted boot. It alarmed him to do so, but he felt, as premier, the duty. First, the noble comment; next, the boot.

He was aware of the fact that the men around him kept glancing from the frozen angel up toward the barely discernible gray clouds. They were wondering, of course, if it could be God-sent. Sounds came to him—bells of churches, litanies recited, chants—Gregorian music in Caucasian bass. To his nostrils came the smell of incense. He thought, as atheists must: What if they were right?

Against that thought he ranged another speedily enough; it was his custom. He wrenched the ears and eyes of his mind from the church pageantry of recollected boyhood, in the Czar's time, to other parts of his expanding domain. He made himself hear temple bells, watch sacred elephants parade, behold the imbecile sacrifices and rituals of the heathen. They, too, were believers, and they had no angels. Angels, he therefore reasoned, were myths.

It occurred to him—it had already been suggested to him by General Mornsk, of Intelligence—that some such being as this, come on a brief visit from an unknown small planet, had given rise to the whole notion of angels. He chuckled.

Vorshiv had the temerity to ask, "You have formed an opinion, comrade?"

The premier stared at the stringy, leathern man with his watery eyes and his record: eighteen million unworthy citizens "subdued." "Certainly." He looked once more at the casualty. "Autopsy it. Then destroy the remains."

"No," a voice murmured.

The premier whirled about. "Who said that?"

It was a young man, the youngest general, one born after 1917, one who had seen no world but the Soviet. Now, pale with horror and shame, the young man said, "I merely thought, sir, to preserve this for study."

"I detected sentiment. Credulity. Superstition. Your protest was a whimper."

The young officer showed a further brief flicker of dissent. "Perhaps—this being cannot be destroyed by our means."

The premier nodded at the body, and his thin, long lips became longer, thinner. A smile, perhaps. "Is not our second test planned for the very near future?"

"Tomorrow," Mornsk said. "But we are prepared to postpone it if you think the situation——"

"Postpone it?" The premier smiled. "On the contrary. Follow plans. Autopsy this animal. Attach what remains to the bomb. That should destroy it effectively." He glanced icily at the young general, made a daub at a salute and tramped over the ice-crisped tundra toward the jeeps.

On the way back to the base, Mornsk, of Intelligence, decided to mention his theory. Mornsk turned in his front seat. "One thing, Comrade. Our American information is not, as you know, what it was. However, we had word this spring of what the British call a 'flap.' Many sudden, very secret conferences. Rumors. We never were able to determine the cause—and the brief state of near-panic among the leadership has abated. Could it be—the 'flap' followed one of their tests—that they, too, had a 'casualty'?"

"It could be," the premier replied. "What of it?"

"Nothing. I merely would have thought, Comrade, that they would have announced it to the world."

The thin lips drew thinner again. "They are afraid. They would, today, keep secret a thousand things that, yesterday, they would have told one another freely. Freedom. Where is it now? We are driving it into limbo—their kind. To limbo." He shut his prune eyes, opened them, turned to the officer on his left. "Gromov, I hope the food's good here. I'm famished."

An old Russian proverb ran through his mind: "Where hangs the smoke of hate burns a fiercer fire called fear."

The trick, he reflected, was to keep that fire of fear alive, but to know at the same time it might consume you also. Then the trick was to make the fear invisible in the smokes of hatred. Having accomplished that, you would own men's souls and your power would be absolute, so long as you never allowed men to see how their hate was but fear, and so long as you, afraid, knowing it, hence more shrewd and cautious than the rest, did not become a corpse at the hands of the hating fearful.

There, in a nutshell, was the recipe for dictatorship. Over the proletariat. Over the godly believers. Over the heathen. Over all men, even those who imagined they were free and yet could be made to hate:

Frighten; then furnish the whipping boys. Then seize. Like governing children.

If more of these angels showed up, he reflected, it would simply be necessary to pretend they were demons, Lucifers, outer-space men bent on assassinating humanity. So simple.

The slate-hued buildings of the base rose over

the tundra. From the frigid outdoors he entered rooms heated to a tropical temperature by the nearby reactors. There, too, the Soviets had somewhat surpassed the free peoples.

His secretary, Maximov, had thoughtfully forwarded Lamenula, to temper the hardships of the premier's Siberian hegira. He was amused, even somewhat stirred, to learn the young lady had objected to the trip, had fought, was even now in a state of alternate hysteria and coma—or simulated coma. A little communist discipline was evidently needed, and being applied; and he would take pleasure in administering the finishing touches.

Late that night he woke up with a feeling of uneasiness. A feeling, he decided, of fear. The room was quiet, the guards were in place, nothing menaced him in the immediate moment, and Lamenula was asleep. Her bruises were beginning to show, but she had learned how to avoid them in the future, which was the use of bruises.

What frightened him was the angel. Church music, which he had remembered, but refused to listen to in his mind, now came back to him. It did not cause him to believe that the visitor had given a new validity to an Old Testament. It had already caused him to speculate that what he, and a billion others, had thitherto regarded as pure myth might actually be founded on scientific fact.

What therefore frightened the premier as he lay on the great bed in the huge, gaudily decorated bedchamber, was an intuition of ignorance. Neither he nor his physicists, he nor his political philosophers—nor any men in the world that still, ludicrously, blindly, referred to itself as "free"—really knew anything fundamental about the universe. Nobody really knew, and could demonstrate scientifically, the "why" of time and space and energy—or matter. The angel—the very beautiful angel that had lain on the cold tundra—might possibly mean and be something that not he nor any living man, skeptic or believer, could even comprehend.

That idea wakened him thoroughly. Here was a brand-new dimension of the unknown to be faced. He sat up, switched on the light and put a cigarette in his thin mouth.

How, he asked himself, could this fear of the unknown be translated into a hatred of something known, and so employed to enhance power? His power. That was, invariably, the formulation; once made, it generally supplied its own answer.

You could not, however, set the people in the Soviets and the people in the rest of the world to hating angels. Not when, especially, their reality—

or real counterpart—could never be exhibited and had become a military secret.

Mornsk's theory bemused him. Had the Americans also shot one down with an H-bomb? If so, they'd followed a procedure like his own, apparently. Saying nothing. Examining the victim, doubtless.

He realized he should go to sleep. He was to be roused early for the test of the next super-H-bomb, but he kept ruminating, as he smoked, on the people of the United States. *Whom,* he reflected, *we shall destroy in millions* in —— The number of months and days remaining before the blitz of the U.S.A. was so immense a secret that he did not let himself reckon it exactly. *Whom we shall slaughter in sudden millions, soon.*

But suppose something intervened? Angels?

He smiled again. Even if such creatures had visited the earth once before, it was long ago. They might be here again now. They would presumably go away again, for millenniums. Ample time to plant the Red flag everywhere in the world.

Still, he could not know, and not to know was alarming.

There was a phone beside his bed. He could astound telephone operators halfway around the world, and yet, doubtless, in ten minutes, fifteen—

perhaps an hour—he could converse with the President of the United States.

"Seen any angels, Mr. President? . . . What do you make of it? . . . Perhaps we aren't as knowing as we imagine. . . . Possibly we should meet and talk things over—postpone any—plans we might have for the near future? At least, until this matter of invading angels is settled."

It wouldn't be that simple or that quick, but it might be done. And it might be that that was the only possible way to save the Soviet, because it might be the one way left to save man and his planet.

He thought about the abandonment of the Communist philosophy, the scrapping of decades of horror and sacrifice, the relaxing of the steely discipline; he thought of the dreams of world domination gone glimmering—of "freedom" being equated with communism. There welled in him the avalanche of hatred which was his essence and the essence of his world. He ground out his cigarette and tried to sleep. . . .

In the morning, after the test shot—which was also very successful and, the premier thought, frightening—he requested the report on the autopsy of the casualty. He had to ask repeatedly, since it became clear that none of the nearby persons—generals, commissars, aides, technicians—wanted to answer. He commanded Mornsk.

The general sweated in the cold air, under a sky again clear and as palely blue as turquoise. "We have no report, Comrade. The autopsy was undertaken last night by Smidz. An ideal man, we felt—the great biologist, who happened to be here, working on radiation effects on pigs. He labored alone all night, and then—your orders, Comrade—the—remains were fixed to the bomb." Mornsk's glance at the towering mushroom disposed of that matter. "It was then discovered that Smidz made no notes of whatever he learned."

"Get Smidz."

"This morning early, Comrade, he killed himself."

General Scott did not return to the Pacific until nearly Christmastime. He had hoped not to go back at all, particularly since he had spent the autumn with his family in Baltimore, commuting weekdays to the Pentagon. In December, however, he received secret information of still another series of springtime nuclear-weapons tests and orders to fly again to the Sangre Islands, where he would prepare another of the group for total sacrifice. The death of islands was becoming commonplace to the weaponeers. In the unfinished span of his own military career, a suitable target had grown from a square of canvas stretched over a wooden frame to a building, and then to a city block, next a city's heart, and now, an island the size of Manhattan. This, moreover, was not holed, wrecked or merely set afire, but wiped off the earth's face, its roots burned away deep into the sea, its substance thrown, poisonous, across the skies.

He went reluctantly, but as a soldier must, aware that by now he had the broadest experience —among general officers—for the task at hand.

Work went ahead with no more than the usual quota of "bugs"—or what his orderly would have called "snafus." It was a matter of "multiple snafu," however, which finally led the general to order a light plane to fly him to Tempest Island. There had arisen an argument with the natives about property rights; there was some trouble with the placement of instruments; a problem about electric power had come up; and a continuing report of bad chow was being turned in from the island mess hall. Time for a high-echelon look-see.

As he flew in, General Scott noticed the changes which he had helped to devise. The mission playing field had been bulldozed big enough to accommodate fair-sized cargo planes on two X-angled strips. Here and there the green rug of jungle had been macheted open to contain new measuring devices of the scientists. The harbor had been deepened; dredged-up coral made a mole against the purple Pacific as well as the foundation for a sizable pier. Otherwise, Tempest was the same.

His mind, naturally, returned to his previous trip and to what had been found on the island. The general had observed a growing tendency, even in Admiral Stanforth and Rawson, now a colonel, to recall the angel more as a figure of a dream than as reality. Just before the landing gear came down he looked for, and saw, the very glade in which the angel had fallen. Its clear spring was an emerald eye and the Bletias were in violet bloom all around.

Then he was on the ground, busy with other officers, busy with the plans and problems of a great nation, scared, arming, ready these days for war at the notice of a moment or at no notice whatever. Even here, thousands upon thousands of miles from the nervous target areas of civilization, the fear and the desperate urgency of man had rolled up, parting the jungle and erecting grim engines associated with ruin.

He was on his way to the headquarters tent when he noticed, and recognized, the young boy.

Teddy Simms, he thought, was about ten now, the age of his own son. But Teddy looked older than ten, and very sad.

The general stepped away from his accompanying officers. "You go on," he said. "I'll soon catch up. This is an old friend of mine." He waved then. "Hi, Ted! Why you all dressed up? Remember me?"

The youngster stopped and did recognize the general, with a look of anxiousness. He nodded and glanced down at his clothes. "I'm gonna leave! Tonight. It'll be"—his face brightened slightly—"my very first airplane ride!"

"That's swell!" The general had been puzzled by signs of apprehension in the boy. "How's your father? And your aunt? Cora, wasn't it?"

"She's O.K. But father——" His lip shook.

Marc Scott no longer smiled. "Your father——"

The boy answered stonily, "Went nuts."

"After——" the general asked, knew the answer and was unsurprised by the boy's increased anxiousness.

"I'm not allowed to say. I'd go to prison forever."

A jeepful of soldiers passed. The general moved to the boy's side and said, "With me, you are, Ted. Because I know all about it, too. I'm—I'm mighty sorry your father—is ill. Maybe he'll recover, though."

"The board doesn't think so. They're giving up the mission. That's why I'm going away. To school,

Stateside. Father"—he fell in step with the general, leaping slightly with each stride—"Father never got any better—after that old day you were here."

"What say, we go back where—it happened? I'd like to see it once more, Ted."

"No." Teddy amended it, "No, sir. I'm not even allowed to talk about it. I don't ever go there!"

"It's too bad. I thought it was the most beautiful thing that ever happened to me in my life."

The boy stared at the man incredulously. "You did? Father thought it was the worst thing ever happened."

"I felt as if you, Ted—and I—all of us—were seeing something completely wonderful!"

The boy's face showed an agreement which changed, slowly, to a pitiable emotion—regret, or fear, perhaps shame. It was the general's intuition which bridged the moment: Teddy knew more than he had ever said about the angel; he had lied originally or omitted something.

"What is it, son?" The general's tone was fatherly.

Eyes darted toward the jungle, back to the general and rested measuringly, then hopelessly. It was as if the youngster had considered aloud running away and had decided his adversary was too powerful to evade.

He stood silent a moment longer; then said

almost incoherently, "I never meant to keep it! But it is gold! And we were always so mighty poor! I thought, for a while, if Father sold it—— But he couldn't even think of things like selling gold books. He had lost his reason."

If the general's heart surged, if his mind was stunned, he did not show it. "Gold books?" His eyes forgave in advance.

"Just one book, but heavy." The dismal boy looked at the ground. "I didn't steal it, really! That angel—dropped it."

The general's effort was tremendous. Not in battle had composure cost him as dear. "You—read it?"

"Huh!" the boy said. "It was in all kinds of other languages. 'Wisdom,' that angel said it was. 'Gathered from our whole galaxy—for Earth.' Did you ever know——" His voice intensified with the question, as if by asking it he might divert attention from his guilt. "Did you know there are other people on other planets of other suns, all around? Maybe Vega, or the North Star, or Rigel, or more likely old Sirius? That angel mentioned a few names. I forget which."

"No. I didn't realize it. And, you say, this book had a message for the people on Earth, written in all languages. Not English, though?"

"I didn't see any English. I saw—like Japanese

and Arabian—and a lot of kinds of alphabets you never heard of—some just dots."

"And you—threw it away?" He asked it easily too.

"Naw. You couldn't do that! It's gold—at least, it looks like gold. All metal pages. It's got hinges, kind of, for every page. I guess it's fireproof and even space-proof, at the least. I didn't throw it away. I hid it under an old rock. Come on. I'll show you."

They returned to the glade. The book lay beneath a flat stone. There had been another the general was never to know about—a book buried beneath a sod hut in Siberia by a peasant who also had intended to sell it, for he, too, had been poor. But the other book, identical, along with the hovel above it, had been reduced to fractions of its atoms by a certain test weapon which had destroyed the body of its bearer.

This one the general picked up with shaking hands, opened and gazed upon with ashen face.

The hot sun of noon illumined the violet orchids around his tailored legs. The boy stood looking up at him, awaiting judgment, accustomed to harshness; and about them was the black and white filigree of tropical forest. With inexpressible amazement, Marc searched page after page of inscriptions in languages unknown, unsuspected until then. It became apparent that there was one message only, very short, said again and again and again, but he did not know what it was until, toward the last pages, he found the tongues of Earth.

A sound was made by the man as he read them —a sound that began with murmurous despair and ended, as comprehension entered his brain, with a note of exultation. For the message of icy space and flaring stars was this: "Love one another."